Mimi,
A Gatinha

Ajlan Atasoy

Illustrated by Miruna Smit

All for Alara,

always

BIGGER WORLD BOOKS

Illustrations by DeveoStudio.com
Translation by BURG Translations

Mimi,
A Gatinha

written by
Ajlan Atasoy

Illustrated by
Miruna Smit

For a short while,
when she was tiny,
Mimi lived alone,
but she was mighty.

Há um certo tempinho,
quando Mimi era pequenina,
vivia sozinha,
mas não era franzina.

One day, she knocked on the door of a house nearby,
and said to the little girl on the other side,
"I can't find food no matter what I try,
Can't I just come inside,
Just for a little while?"

Certo dia, bateu na porta de uma casa próxima,
e se deparou com uma garotinha,
"Não encontro comida, que lástima,
Posso entrar em sua casa,
Só um minuto já me agrada."

One day, she knocked on the door of a house nearby,
and said to the little girl on the other side,
"I can't find food no matter what I try,
Can't I just come inside,
Just for a little while?"

Certo dia, bateu na porta de uma casa próxima,
e se deparou com uma garotinha,
"Não encontro comida, que lástima,
Posso entrar em sua casa,
Só um minuto já me agrada."

The little girl had lots of curls and a big heart.
She gave the kitty some food and gained her trust.
"Mama!" she said, "we have to take her in!
It's cold and a snowstorm is approaching."
Her mama said, "Oh, sweetheart,
cats make your papa cough and sneeze.
But I know just the person
who could put our minds at ease."

A garotinha tinha belos cachos e um grande coração.
Ela deu comida à gatinha e ganhou sua adoração.
"Mamãe!", disse ela, "temos que deixá-la entrar!"
"Tem uma tempestade vindo e o frio pode congelar."
E a mãe disse, "ah, querida, os gatos fazem seu pai espirrar e tossir,"
"mas eu conheço a pessoa certa que pode nos acudir."

That night, the kitten slept in a warm home,
Which she only left with her new and forever mom.
"I'll call her Minnosh," her new mom said
Because the kitten had an "M" on her forehead.
Later that name became "Mimi"
Because saying "Mimiiii" is so easy.

Naquela noite, a gatinha dormiu em uma casa aquecida,
da qual só saiu com sua nova mamãe querida.
Sua nova mãe disse, "Vai se chamar Marina",
porque a gatinha tinha um "M" em sua adorável testinha.
Depois se tornou "Mimi",
porque dizer "Mimiii" é muito mais fácil.

A short while later,
when Mimi turned one,
Mimi and Mom moved to a distant land,
They crossed an ocean, then a river,
then they crossed the ocean back again.

Após um tempo, quando Mimi fez um ano,
Ela e Mamãe mudaram-se para terras distantes,
atravessaram um oceano, um rio, e de novo o oceano.

Mimi hated planes, but such lovely songs the birds sang.
In those lovely gardens, Mimi took long naps.

Mimi odiava aviões, mas os pássaros cantavam tão belas canções,
naqueles belos jardins, Mimi tirava longos cochilos.

Then one day,
on a cold winter's night,
a beautiful baby girl arrived.
Yes, that was me, and I was so loved.
Mom looked big, and sleepy, and tired,
Yet, happier than she'd ever been.
Seeing all that joy, Mimi was keen.

Até que um dia,
em uma noite de inverno fria,
chegou uma linda bebezinha.
Sim, era eu, e fui tão amada.
Mamãe parecia grande, sonolenta e exausta.
Mas nunca estivera tão extasiada.
E Mimi, vendo tanta alegria, ficava entusiasmada.

As I grew bigger, so did Mimi's love.
Even when I brought home a rabbit,
Mimi stayed gentle, loving, and kind.
The way Mimi saw it,
everyone needed a warm house
On a cold winter's night.

O amor de Mimi aumentava conforme eu crescia.
Mesmo quando levei um coelho para casa,
Mimi continuou gentil, amável e grata.
Do mesmo jeito que a Mimi,
todos merecem uma casa quentinha
em uma noite de inverno fria.

Meet
Ajlan Atasoy

Ajlan, formerly known as Dr. Atasoy, lives amongst lovely trees in central New Jersey, USA. When Ajlan is not busy researching and developing new medicines to treat difficult illnesses, she loves playing and learning with her daughter, who is the inspiration behind Bigger World Books. Ajlan and her daughter's love for animals, adventures, and each other inspired this book. We hope you love it.

About

BIGGER WORLD BOOKS

Ajlan adores how immense a young child's capacity is to learn languages without prejudice. She formed Bigger World Books LLC to create children's books not only for English-speaking bookworms, but also for their multilingual loved ones or educators. Each story comes with bilingual versions with culturally relevant translations.

As a Turkish native raising her family in the USA, Ajlan noticed that multicultural families need more bilingual books to connect with loved ones, whether over a bedtime story with granma (or "anneanne"), working in the garden with grandpa ("dede"), or singing a song in each other's language with Auntie Ceren. Because having a different mother's tongue is a gift.

Also Available:

Mimi the Cat (English)
Kedi Mimi (Turkish-English)
La Gata Mimí (Spanish-English; Latin America)
Das Kätzchen Mimi (German-English)

More bilingual books coming soon!